Three Little Kittens

Distributed by The Child's World®
1980 Lookout Drive • Mankato, MN 56003-1705
800-599-READ • www.childsworld.com

Acknowledgments
The Child's World®: Mary Berendes, Publishing Director
The Design Lab: Kathleen Petelinsek, Design

Library of Congress Cataloging-in-Publication Data
Weidner, Teri.
 Three little kittens / illustrated by Teri Weidner.
    p. cm.
 ISBN 978-1-60954-285-6 (library bound: alk. paper)
 1. Nursery rhymes. 2. Children's poetry. [1. Nursery rhymes.] I. Title.
 PZ8.3.W417Th 2011
 398.8—dc22
 [E]   2010032420

Printed in the United States of America in Mankato, Minnesota.
December 2010
PA02073

ILLUSTRATED BY TERI WEIDNER

Three little kittens,
they lost their mittens,
and they began to cry.
"Oh mother dear,
we sadly fear,
that we have lost our mittens."

4

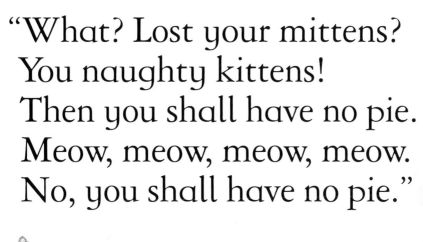

"What? Lost your mittens?
You naughty kittens!
Then you shall have no pie.
Meow, meow, meow, meow.
No, you shall have no pie."

The three little kittens,
they found their mittens,
and they began to cry.
"Oh mother dear!
See here! See here!
We have found our mittens."

"What? Found your mittens?
You silly kittens!
Then you shall have some pie.
Purr, purr, purr, purr.
Yes, you shall have some pie."

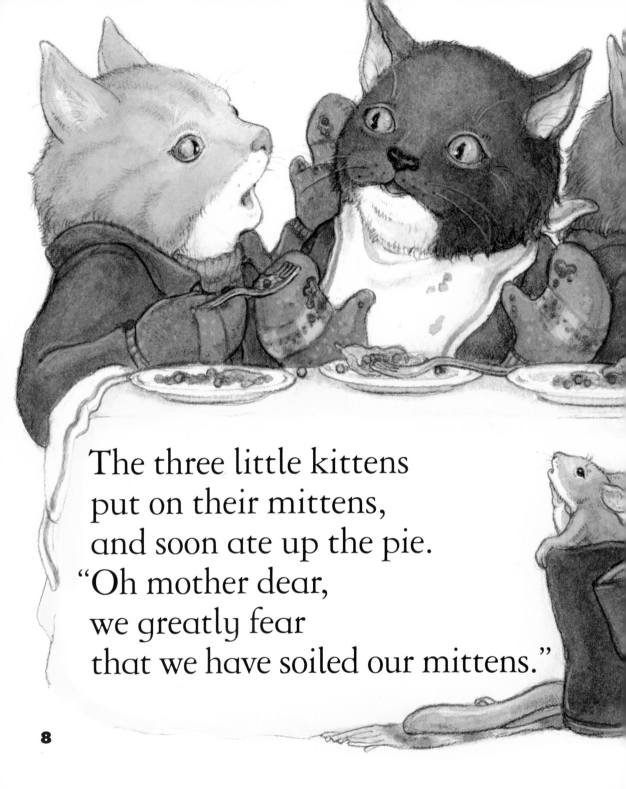

The three little kittens
put on their mittens,
and soon ate up the pie.
"Oh mother dear,
we greatly fear
that we have soiled our mittens."

"What? Soiled your mittens?
You naughty kittens!"
Then they began to sigh,
"Meow, meow, meow, meow."
Then they began to sigh.

9

The three little kittens,
they washed their mittens,
and hung them out to dry.
"Oh mother dear!
Look here! Look here!
We have washed our mittens."

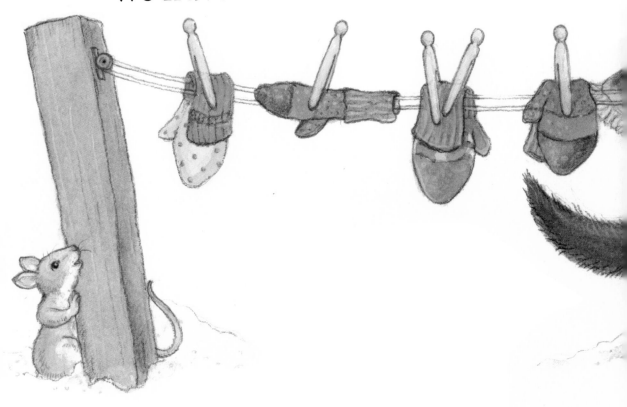

"What? Washed your mittens?
Such good little kittens.
But I smell a mouse close by!
Hush, hush, hush, hush.
I smell a mouse close by."

ABOUT MOTHER GOOSE

We all remember the Mother Goose nursery rhymes we learned as children. But who was Mother Goose, anyway? Did she even exist? The answer is . . . we don't know! Many different tales surround this famous name.

Some people think she might be based on Goose-footed Bertha, a kindly old woman in French legend who told stories to children. The inspiration for this legend might have been Queen Bertha of France, who died in 783 and whose son Charlemagne ruled much of Europe. Queen Bertha was called Big-footed Bertha or Queen Goosefoot because one foot was larger than the other.

The name "Mother Goose" first appeared in Charles Perrault's *Les Contes de ma Mère l'Oye* ("Tales of My Mother Goose"), published in France in 1697. This was a collection of fairy tales including "Cinderella" and "Sleeping Beauty"—but these were stories, not poems. The first published Mother Goose nursery rhymes appeared in England in 1781, as *Mother Goose's Melody; or Sonnets for the Cradle.* But some of the verses themselves are hundreds of years old, passed along by word of mouth.

Although we don't really know the origins of Mother Goose or her nursery rhymes, we *do* know that these timeless verses are beloved by children everywhere!

ABOUT THE ILLUSTRATOR

Teri Weidner grew up in Fairport, New York, where she spent much of her free time drawing horses and other animals. Today, she is delighted to have a career illustrating books for children. She lives in Portsmouth, New Hampshire with her husband and a menagerie of pets.